For Our Turtle Dream Team

Amy, Amelia, David & Brett

RHH & TF

An imprint of Bonnier Publishing Group
853 Broadway, New York, New York 10003
Text copyright © 2011 by Bee Productions, Inc.
Illustration copyright © 2011 by Tor Freeman
First published in the UK by Templar Publishing.
This little bee books edition, 2015.
All rights reserved, including the right of
reproduction in whole or in part in any form.
LITTLE BEE BOOKS is a trademark of
Bonnier Publishing Group, and associated
colophon is a trademark of Bonnier Publishing Group.
Manufactured in China 1214 008
Library of Congress Control Number: 2014943631
First Edition 2 4 6 8 10 9 7 5 3 1
ISBN 978-1-4998-0046-3

www.littlebeebooks.com
www.bonnierpublishing.com

Turtle and Me

ROBIE H. HARRIS

Illustrated by

TOR FREEMAN

LITTLE BEE BOOKS

I met Turtle on the day I was born.
On that great and important day, I was totally tiny
and Turtle was way bigger than me.

Now I'm way bigger than Turtle. But that doesn't matter.
We're best friends. We've been together forever.

Way back when I was a little baby,
I smiled every time I put my arms
around Turtle.

And every time
I rubbed Turtle's tummy,
I laughed.

Back when I was
a bigger baby, I *had* to
have Turtle around.

But as soon as I
could hold Turtle,
I stopped yelling.

Every single time
Mommy left the room,
I yelled *Waaaaaaah!*

Holding Turtle made me
feel okay again.

When I was still a little kid and had to take
a nap, sometimes I felt lonely and sad.

But as soon as I snuggled up with my soft and
cuddly Turtle, I didn't feel lonely or sad anymore.

Turtle's a lot older now. And so am I. But I still like to have Turtle around.

And sometimes I still like to hold Turtle. But now Turtle's colors aren't all that bright. And Turtle's ripped, raggedy, and old. Some bad things happened to Turtle.

When I was still very little,
I dumped a whole bowl
of spaghetti on my head.
That gooey, slippery
spaghetti slid down my chin
and onto Turtle. The two
of us had yucky orange
spots all over us.

Last year, our puppy, Pooch,
chewed a giant hole right
in the middle of Turtle's shell.

This year, after I ate a big piece of Mommy's birthday cake, and the candy rose on top, and a huge scoop of chocolate marshmallow crunch ice cream . . .

I threw up all over Turtle.

When anything that bad happens
to Turtle, I feel so awful that
sometimes I even cry. And I bet
Turtle feels awful too.

But when bad things happen,
I always make sure that Turtle
gets sewn up, washed up,
fixed up—and is okay again.

TURTLE
REPAIR KIT

Last month, I left Turtle at the park.
That was the worst! I thought I would
never ever see or hold Turtle again.
Mommy and I ran back to the park.
I cried the whole way.

But Turtle was still there!
At the bottom of the slide,
all covered in mud,
with gum on one foot,
and two new rips.

So I carried Turtle
all the way home,
even though Turtle felt
soooo *grrross*!

Back home, we tried to wash off the icky-sticky part and the slimy-muddy part.

But Turtle was still *grrross*.

So we sewed up the rips, gave Turtle a bath, and put Turtle in the dryer.

After all that,
I gave Turtle
the biggest hug.
And I decided
for sure that
I would never let
anything bad
happen to Turtle
ever again.

But then—the worst thing of all happened.

Last Friday my friend and I sailed around the world.

Turtle was the Captain, so Turtle steered the ship.

But my friend said *she* wanted to steer the ship, and she grabbed Turtle from me. I said that Turtle was still the Captain, and I grabbed Turtle back.

Now Turtle had the biggest, baddest,

most gigantic, horrible rip ever!

"You ripped my Turtle!" I yelled.
"Having Turtle's a BABY thing!"
yelled my friend.
"I'm not a baby! I'm a pirate!"
I yelled back.

"Well, I'm going home!"
yelled my friend.
And she did.

I hugged Turtle tight.

The rip was so big that almost all the stuffing in Turtle's tummy fell out. "Ohhhh, poor Turtle!" I cried.

I stuffed the stuffing back inside as fast as I could and taped Turtle's tummy back together.

But now Turtle looked ugly.
So I left my ripped-up, ugly old
Turtle on the floor. I didn't
need Turtle anymore.

At bedtime, Daddy
brought me Turtle.
"But Daddy," I said, "I don't
want Turtle anymore…"
"Okay," he said. "I'll put
Turtle back on the floor."

Mommy turned out the light.

I shut my eyes very tight.

I hugged my pillow.

I counted to seventy-seven.

I sang a song.

I squeezed my
eyes tighter.
And then
I yelled,

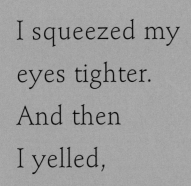

Daddy came in. "Do you want Turtle?" he asked.

"NO!" I said. "Having Turtle's a baby thing! And I'm BIG!

And I'm getting bigger!

So I don't need Turtle ever again!"

"You are very big now," said Daddy, "but not *all* big. Not just yet." Then he grabbed Turtle and flopped down on my bed. Daddy rubbed Turtle's nose and pretended to snore.

That made me giggle.

Then I rubbed Turtle's tummy and pretended to snore.
And that made Daddy laugh. Even though I was very
big now, holding Turtle still felt pretty good.
"Night-night, my big boy," whispered Daddy.
"Night-night, my Daddy," I whispered.

"And night-night, my good-old, chewed-up,
sewn-up, taped-up, ripped-up, raggedy Turtle."
Before I could count to thirty-three,
I fell asleep. And I think Turtle did too.